coche
cótchay

flores
flórayss

paella
pie-élyah

máquina fotográfica
máckeenah fotográficah

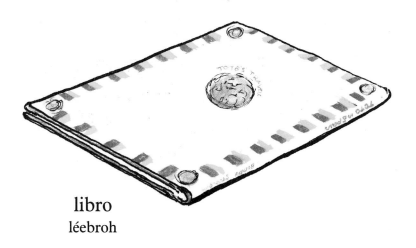

libro
léebroh

naranja
naránhah

Thought you would enjoy learning about our spaniard part of our heritage

Hope you enjoy it!

Love Renaldo & Kim

Toto in Spain

BIDDY STREVENS

A first taste of Spain
and the Spanish language

PASSPORT BOOKS
a division of *NTC Publishing Group*
Lincolnwood, Illinois USA

This edition first published in 1992 by Passport Books,
a division of NTC Publishing Group,
4255 West Touhy Avenue, Lincolnwood (Chicago),
Illinois 60646–1975 U.S.A.

Originally published by
Little, Brown and Company (UK) Limited.

Library of Congress Catalog Number 92–60802

FOR MY MOTHER

Typeset by Florencetype Ltd, Kewstoke, Avon
Colour separations by Fotographics, Hong Kong
Printed and bound in Belgium by Proost, Turnhout

"Grandpa!" Toto shouts, as they walk down the *Ramblas* in Barcelona. "Please stand still a minute. You'll come out all fuzzy if you keep moving like that!"

"Catch me if you can!" laughs Toto's grandfather.

"Why won't anyone stand still in this place?" asks Toto as a flamenco dancer whirls past him, stamping her feet and clicking her castanets.

"¡*Olé!*" cries the dancer. "Take a picture of us!"

"I would if you'd only stand still," says Toto dismally, looking around in vain for his grandfather.

"Would you like to be a jungle explorer?" calls Grandpa from behind some potted plants at a stand.

"I thought I'd lost you," says Toto, his camera ready. "Please wait!"

"No waiting in the jungle allowed!" cries Grandpa. "Who knows what might be lurking around the next bush?"

"Whoops!" Grandpa bumps into a painting on an easel. The artist scowls at him.

"Is that the *Ramblas* you're painting?" Grandpa continues. "It looks a little fuzzy to me. . . ."

"We'd better get going!" Grandpa tells Toto. "We're going on a tour of Spain this afternoon. . . ."

"A tour of Spain?" asks Toto in surprise. "I thought we were visiting Barcelona. Spain's enormous!"

"You'll see. Follow me – our first stop's the market."

"Would you like some toasted almonds – *almendras tostadas*?" asks Grandpa. "Or perhaps you'd prefer some *turrón* – almond candy?"

"Both please, er, *por favor*," replies Toto.

"If you can count to three, we'll buy some oranges too," says Grandpa.

"*Uno, dos, tres*," says Toto proudly.

"*Tres naranjas, por favor*," Grandpa asks the fruit seller. "Now we're all set. Off we go to the cable car!"

They climb into a cable car that lifts them high over Barcelona, and Grandpa sings at the top of his voice,

"Oh, I love a ride in a cable car,
Oh, I love a ride beside the sea,
Oh, there's nothing so spectacular
As a ride in a cable car,
But it all looks like *paella* to me!"

"Silly Grandpa, just because we had *paella* for lunch!" Toto laughs.
"Wow! I can see the *Ramblas*, and some ships and. . . ."
"Well I can't!" snorts Grandpa. "Have a *naranja*!"

"This is where our tour of Spain begins, Toto," says Grandpa. "Beyond these castle gates are houses from every region of Spain. And my very best *amigos* are inside waiting to meet you! Remember to say *buenos días* to them all."

"Only if you promise to let me take a picture of you somewhere!" replies Toto firmly.

"Conchita, this is my grandson!" says Grandpa proudly.

"*¡Buenos días!*" says Toto, trying to take another photo.

"What a fine boy!" Conchita smiles. "I want you to have this small souvenir of your first visit to Spain."

"*¡Olé!*" cries Grandpa. "Real castanets! Now say *muchas gracias*, Toto."

"Phew, it's hot!" says Grandpa as he drags Toto to the other end of the *Pueblo Español*. "But Manuel will have some hats to protect us from the sun. *Dos sombreros, por favor*, Manuel. One for me and one for my grandson here. Toto . . .? That's funny, where's he gone?"

"*Buenos días*," says a muffled voice from inside a big *sombrero*.

"*Buenos días*," says Toto again.

"*Hola*," smiles Jordi, shaking Toto's hand.

"Jordi, can you show Toto how to play the castanets?" asks Grandpa, with a flourish and a stamp of his feet.

"*¡Olé!*" shouts Jordi. "Hold the castanets like this. That's it – click-clack!"

Toto and his grandfather continue their tour of the Spanish Village, nibbling almonds and looking for a place to take the photo that Grandpa has at last promised to pose for.

"This is the perfect spot!" cries Toto excitedly, climbing up onto a wall.

"Now don't move, Grandpa!"

But when Toto looks through his camera, Grandpa has disappeared once again.

"COME BACK, GRANDPA!" he cries in despair, searching the crowd of tourists. "You promised. I don't want to play hide-and-seek again!"

Old Jordi comes hobbling up to Toto. "What is your grandfather up to? He just shot past my shop – zoooommm – like an Olympic runner!"

"I think it's because he doesn't like having his photo taken," says Toto sadly.

"*Amigos* – come quickly," pants Manuel. "I think the sun has gone to Grandpa's head. I asked him where he was going so fast, but he didn't even turn around. He looked very angry. We must stop him. He went that way!"

"Toto!" cries Conchita in surprise. "What are YOU doing back here? Your grandfather just ran past, and I thought he was chasing you – just think, at his age!"

"He's run away," cries Toto, "and left me all alone!"

"He couldn't have run away, and you're not alone!" Conchita comforts him. "Jordi, Manuel, and I will help you find him. Quick let's follow him! I heard him calling for a taxi outside the gates!"

"Look! There he goes, around that corner. Hurry, driver, follow that taxi!" shouts Conchita.

"Honk, honk!" goes Toto's taxi, all the way around Barcelona. "Beep, beep!" goes Grandpa's taxi.

"Why are all those drivers waving their fists at us?" asks Toto.

"Because we're getting in their way," Manuel replies, waving his fist back.

  "He's stopped outside the *Parque Güell*," says Conchita.

Conchita has to pay the taxi driver, and by the time Toto reaches the steps,
Grandpa has disappeared once again.

  "*¿Dónde está?*" cries Manuel. "Where is he?"

"Did you see an old man run past here?" Jordi asks a tourist.

"Hey, look!" cries Toto, bending down in front of a peculiar statue. "Here are the rest of Grandpa's almonds, and his last orange. There must be a hole in his bag. . . ."

"More *almendras* here – he went this way!" cries Conchita.

The rescue party follows the trail of almonds all the way to the top of the steps.

"No more *almendras*. What will we do now?" wonders Jordi.

"*¡No comprendo!*" says Toto, looking through a park telescope. "I don't understand how this works. All I can see is sky."

"Point it lower down!" says Manuel. "Below my hand. . . ."

"Here, let me have a look!" Manuel continues.

"Wait, I can see him!" cries Toto. "He's over there on the terrace, and he needs help!"

"*¡Ay, ay, ay!*" Toto and his *amigos* hear Grandpa shouting as they run to the scene.

"Stop! That's my grandfather! *Por favor*, PLEASE STOP!" shouts Toto, completely out of breath.

"Toto! Thank goodness you found me!" pants Grandpa. "You see *Señora*," he tells an extremely angry grandmother shaking her walking stick, "this is MY grandchild, Toto, and I'm very proud of him, so why would I want to steal YOUR grandchild?"

"Well, why did you chase us like that? I've never been so frightened – my poor heart," she replies, trembling all over.

"*Señora*, allow me!" says Manuel, sitting her down on his tiny chair.

"Let me play some pleasing notes on my guitar," says Jordi, "to soothe your troubled nerves."

"*Me llamo* Tina," the little girl tells Toto.

"*Me llamo* Toto and I don't think I look at all like you!" Toto laughs. "But we ARE both wearing the same color clothes, and we've both got hats!" Toto and Tina burst out laughing.

"*Lo siento, Señora,*" says Grandpa, bowing as low as he can before Tina's grandmother. "I'm so sorry I frightened you. Tina looks just like Toto to me. I need to get my eyes tested!"

"That's all right. I can see now that *Señor* is no kidnapper," the old lady replies.

"Keep still, everyone!" calls Toto. "*Uno, dos, tres.* . . . Click, at last – the perfect photo of Grandpa with all my new *amigos*!"

mantón
mantón

bolso
bólssoh

niña
néenyah

silla
séelyah

guitarra
gueetárrah

turrón
toorrón

*In Latin America and parts of Spain